For Zoe ~ S. S.

For Clare ~ C. P.

tiger tales
5 River Road, Suite 128, Wilton, CT 06897
Published in the United States 2018
Originally published in Great Britain 2018
by Little Tiger Press
Text copyright © 2018 Suzy Senior
Illustrations copyright © 2018 Claire Powell
ISBN-13: 978-1-68010-097-6
ISBN-10: 1-68010-097-1
Printed in China
LTP/1400/2201/0318

For more insight and activities, visit us at www.tigertalesbooks.com

OCTOPANTS

by Suzy Senior • Illustrated by Claire Powell

tiger tales

Hello there! I'm an octopus.
There's something you should know . . .

I don't have any underpants.
I have nothing on below!

I tried to buy some octopants.
I tried all over town.

Clam Closet

But everyone just laughed and laughed,
Or answered with a frown . . .

BARGAIN
☆
BUCKET

"Underpants? For you?" they said.
"Oh, no. We don't have ANY.
The problem seems to be your legs—
You just have six too many!"

I've even tried to shop online.
I tried to surf the net.
I found a cod, three tuna,
And my credit card got wet!

I still could NOT find octopants.
It almost made me cry.
Everyone has underpants,
Except for octopi.

But then one day I found a place
I hadn't seen before.
A seahorse hovered just inside
The huge revolving door.

"Good morning! Can I help you, sir?
Why don't you step inside?
My Under-Sea Emporium
Is famous ocean-wide.

"I have bobble hats
for barnacles . . .

And evening wear for eels . . .

Onesies just for urchins . . .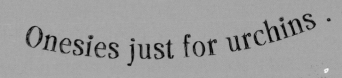

And slipper socks for seals.

Water wings for whales . . .

And rainbow paint for rainbow trout
To brighten up their scales.

"Yes! I have clothes for EVERYONE,
     With spots and stripes and rockets,
Pirate ships and sparkly bits,
     And lots of handy pockets!

"Now . . . underwear for you, sir?
I think you've been misled.
Perhaps you don't need octopants
But something else instead . . . ."

And then I saw the problem.
I'd looked at this all wrong.
These legs weren't legs.
These legs were ARMS,
And had been, all along!

Hello there! I'm an octopus,
And now my day is better:
Instead of buying underpants,

CHANGING ROOM
MAXIMUM 8 LEGS

I bought an
OCTO-SWEATER!